Hamsters Don't Glow in the Dark

by Trina Wiebe

Illustrations
by Marisol Sarrazin

Lobster Press™

To my grandparents, Lorne and Hazel Fletcher.
May the water always be calm and the fish always hungry.

Lobster Press™
1620 Sherbrooke St. West, Suites C & D
Montréal, Québec H3H 1C9
Tel. (514) 904-1101 • Fax (514) 904-1101
www.lobsterpress.com • www.abbyandtess.com

Distribution:

In the United States
Advanced Global Distribution Services
5880 Oberlin Drive
San Diego, CA 92121

In Canada
Raincoast Books
9050 Shaughnessey Street
Vancouver, BC V6P 6E5

We acknowledge the financial support of the Government of Canada through the Book Publishing Industry Development Program (BPIDP) for our publishing activities.

We acknowledge the support of the Canada Council for the Arts for our publishing program.

Canadian Cataloguing in Publication Data
Wiebe, Trina, 1970-
(Abby and Tess, Pet-Sitters™; 4)
ISBN 1-894222-15-6

I. Sarrazin, Marisol, 1965- II. Title.
III. Series: Wiebe, Trina, 1970- Abby and Tess, Pet-Sitters™; 4.

PS8595.I358H34 2000 jC813'.6 C00-900844-6
PZ7.W6349Ha2000

Edited by Jane Pavanel
Cover design by Marielle Maheu
Book design by Geneviève Mayers
Printed and bound in Canada

Contents

1 Mission Impossible 1

2 Abby Needs a Plan 7

3 Blabbermouth Strikes Again 13

4 Hope 17

5 Like Father, Like Son? 21

6 Mr. Bumblebee 25

7 Homeward Bound 31

8 A New Roommate 35

9 Tess Makes a Friend 39

10 A Present for Mr. Nibbles 45

11 Someone Is Forgotten 51

12 Hide and Seek 57

13 A Ghostly Green Glow 63

14 An Amazing Discovery 69

15 The More the Merrier 73

16 Back to School 79

17 A Brilliant Idea 85

1 Mission Impossible

"Isn't he adorable?" Abby asked her friend Rachel. She poked her finger through the bars of the cage and tried to pet the furry brown ball. "He's so round and cute."

"I'd watch it if I were you," warned Rachel. "Don't you remember why we called him Mr. Nibbles?"

Abby laughed, but she withdrew her finger just in case. Mr. Nibbles was the class hamster. He chewed on everything: the bars of his cage, pencils and carrots, even fingers. In the two weeks since Mr. Nibbles had joined Mrs. Hernandez's grade five class, three kids had been nipped by the rodent's sharp teeth.

"He has to chew on stuff," said Abby, remembering what she'd read in a library book. "His teeth never stop growing. Chewing keeps them from getting too long."

"Whatever," said Rachel, looking bored. "You do realize he's just a big, hairy mouse, don't you? My bubby had a mouse in her house and it got in her cupboards and chewed up all her food. It was totally gross."

Abby had been to Rachel's grandmother's house. The kitchen was spotless. A mouse would definitely not have been welcome. Anyway, Abby knew Rachel didn't share her enthusiasm for animals. She was afraid of being bitten or pooped on or something.

"I still think he's adorable," Abby said, wishing Mr. Nibbles would wake up and do something interesting. "Besides, I kind of like mice."

Rachel stuck out her tongue. "Yuck!"

"Okay class, settle down please."

Abby looked up to see the teacher standing by the blackboard at the front of the classroom. She and Rachel hurried to their desks. One by one the students dropped into their seats and the room grew quiet.

"As you know, tomorrow is the last day of school before spring break," Mrs. Hernandez began. Almost immediately her words were met by cheers and hoots from Dirk Kaefermann and some of his friends. They were the noisiest kids in class.

Mrs. Hernandez waited until she had everyone's attention before speaking again. "Which means you'll all have a week off. It also means I need a volunteer to look after Mr. Nibbles for the week."

Abby's hand shot up. "I'll do it," she said excitedly. "I'll take good care of him. I'm a professional pet-sitter, you know."

Mrs. Hernandez looked surprised. "A professional pet-sitter?"

Abby nodded enthusiastically. "That's right. I have my own business and my sister Tess helps me. We take care of all kinds of animals when people have to go away."

"It's true," piped up Rachel. "Once they looked after a lizard named Angus."

"We've taken care of goldfish too, and a pot-bellied pig," said Abby quickly, before Rachel could explain how Angus had ended up wearing Tantalizing Tangerine lip gloss. She didn't want Mrs. Hernandez to think she wasn't responsible.

"Really?" Her teacher seemed impressed. "What an enterprising idea, Abby. What made you decide to start your own business?"

"I love animals," Abby answered simply.

It was true. All she'd ever wanted was a pet of her own. A furry little friend to play with and love. Unfortunately, the apartment building her family lived in didn't allow pets.

Abby thought the No Pets Allowed rule was totally unfair. They allowed kids, didn't they? Kids were noisy and messy and smelly. And sometimes they acted weird.

Take her little sister Tess, for example. Tess was the weirdest kid in the whole building. Most of the time she thought she was a dog. She barked and growled and her favorite toy was a rubber bone. If a building allowed kids, reasoned Abby, they should definitely allow pets.

"I think we've found our volunteer," said Mrs. Hernandez with a smile. She put a yellow sheet of paper on Abby's desk. "Just have your mom fill in this permission slip and you can take Mr. Nibbles home after school tomorrow."

Abby gulped. Take Mr. Nibbles home? She hadn't realized he'd have to come home with her. What about the No Pets Allowed rule?

She opened her mouth to say she couldn't do it, but Mrs. Hernandez was already busy assigning math homework. Abby knew she didn't like to be interrupted. Besides, it would look silly to refuse to take Mr. Nibbles home after bragging to the whole class about being a pet-sitter.

She fingered the yellow slip of paper. She really, really wanted to have Mr. Nibbles for the week. It would be so much fun to look after an animal that actually had fur. But it was impossible.

Or was it?

2 Abby Needs a Plan

Abby thought about Mr. Nibbles all the way home. What was she going to do? She really wanted to pet-sit him. It didn't even matter that she wouldn't get paid. The money wasn't important. It would be so much fun to finally take care of an animal she could play with and cuddle.

But how could she make it happen? Maybe she could sneak Mr. Nibbles into the bedroom she shared with Tess. But I'd never be able to hide him for a whole week, Abby thought with a sigh. Mom and Dad would hear him or smell him or Tess would let it slip. One way or another they'd find out, and then she'd be in big trouble. They might never let her pet-sit again.

It wasn't worth the risk. There must be another way. If only she could think of a plan . . . .

"Look what I've got," Tess said abruptly. She hopped over a crack in the sidewalk and hurried to catch up to Abby. Every day the girls walked to and from school together. It was a rule their parents insisted on.

Tess shoved her hand up close to Abby's nose. "See?"

"That's nice," Abby said, barely glancing at her sister.

"You didn't even look at it." Tess sounded hurt.

"I did so." Abby brushed Tess's hand aside. "It's a bracelet. Big deal."

"No, silly," giggled Tess. "This is for an animal. It's a necklace. Like a flea collar, you know?"

"Right," said Abby absently. "A flea collar for an animal."

"Miki gave it to me," said Tess. Miki Nakama was Tess's best friend. His dad, Jeremy, owned the pet store near their apartment building. She twirled the small greenish-white hoop on her finger. It spun faster and faster until it was a blur.

Abby was still thinking about Mr. Nibbles.

Maybe she could put him in the laundry room in the basement. She could sneak downstairs to feed him and clean his cage. Nobody would hear him down there.

"It glows in the dark," Tess offered hopefully.

"Uh huh."

Suddenly the bracelet flew off of Tess's finger. It hit the sidewalk, bounced several times, then rolled into the street. Tess let out a sharp bark and ran after it.

"Hey!" exclaimed Abby, instantly alert. "Look out!" She leapt after Tess and grabbed her by the arm.

Tess yelped in surprise as Abby dragged her back onto the sidewalk.

"Are you crazy?" gasped Abby. "You didn't even check for cars. You could have been killed!"

Tess pointed at her bracelet. "But . . ."

Abby interrupted her. "Don't you realize you can't just run into the street?"

As the oldest, Abby was in charge of

watching over Tess on the walk home from school. If Tess ever got hurt, her parents would never forgive her. But how could she be responsible for a kid who dashed into the traffic whenever she felt like it?

"My flea collar," protested Tess.

Abby stared at her, not understanding. "What are you talking about?"

"You never listen to me," growled Tess. With exaggerated care she stood on the curb and looked one way, then the other. Then, shooting Abby a haughty look, she stepped into the street and retrieved her bracelet.

"Don't be dumb," scolded Abby. Sometimes it was a real pain being in charge of Tess. What crazy thing would she do next?

Tess shoved the bracelet deep into her pocket. "Sorry," she grumbled, not meeting Abby's eye.

Abby saw her sister's expression and relented. "Just remember for next time, okay? You have to pay attention, you know."

Tess scowled at the sidewalk. "You don't

pay attention to me," she muttered.

Abby didn't answer. She was already thinking about something else. Mr. Nibbles, to be exact. The yellow permission slip in her backpack seemed to rustle in her ear as they walked. There was no way she could give it to Mom. She knew exactly what Mom would say. Rules were rules. No pets allowed.

But sometimes rules could be bent, couldn't they?

3 Blabbermouth Strikes Again

Abby and Tess trudged up the stairs to their apartment in silence. When they reached number 18 Abby tried the doorknob, but the door was locked.

Still thinking about Mr. Nibbles, Abby reached inside the collar of her shirt and pulled out a long string. A copper-colored key dangled from it. Deftly, she slipped the key into the lock and turned the knob.

"I'm hungry," announced Tess as soon as they stepped inside. Both backpacks hit the floor with a thud. Ignoring Tess, Abby tucked the key back inside her shirt. It always hung around her neck, except at night when she slept.

The apartment was empty. Mom must have been held up at work. It didn't happen often, but when it did, it was Abby's job to make sure Tess got her after-school snack. Today all Abby could think about was Mr. Nibbles.

"I'm hungry," complained Tess again,

louder this time. Her voice rose in a whine. "I want a snack."

"Why don't you watch TV?" snapped Abby. She knelt down and unzipped her back-pack. "Mom will be home in a few minutes."

Abby rummaged around for the yellow permission slip. She pulled it out and tried to smooth away the wrinkles. She sighed. There was no way Mom would let her bring home a hamster. It was hopeless.

"Arrroooooo, arrroooooo."

Abby's head jerked up. Tess was standing in the hallway, her eyes scrunched shut. Her chin was tilted toward the ceiling and she was yowling like a dog under a full moon. Abby clapped her hands over her ears and the yellow piece of paper fluttered to the floor.

"What's wrong?" Abby shouted at her sister. She took one hand off her ear long enough to reach over and give Tess a push. "Hey, knock it off!"

Tess glared at Abby. "You never listen to me. I'm hungry!"

"Eat an apple or something," Abby said impatiently. "I've got more important things to worry about right now. Like figuring out how to tell my teacher I can't look after Mr. Nibbles next week."

Tess perked up. "Mr. Nibbles?"

"He's our class hamster," Abby explained. "I told Mrs. Hernandez I'd look after him during spring break, but I didn't realize he'd have to come home with me. How am I going to tell her I can't do it? The whole class will laugh at me."

"Ask Mom," Tess suggested helpfully. "She always knows what to do."

Abby scowled at her. "Yeah, right. Mom can't help me. A rule's a rule. And if I bug her about a pet one more time, she'll probably ground me for a month." She headed for the living room. "Hey, maybe I could tell Mrs. Hernandez that you're allergic to hamsters," she called over her shoulder.

Tess followed Abby. "But I'm not allergic to anything," she said.

"I know that," sighed Abby. Sometimes Tess could be so dense. She threw herself on the couch and stared at the wall. "But I have no choice. What else can I do?"

Tess shrugged. "I still think you should tell Mom about it."

"Tell Mom about what?" asked a voice from the hallway.

4 Hope

When Tess heard Mom's voice she raced to the front hall to greet her. By the time Abby got there, Tess was running around Mom like a dog chasing its tail.

"Well, I'm glad to see you too!" Mom said, kneeling down to catch Tess in her arms and give her a hug. She smiled at Abby. "What did you want to ask me?"

Abby tried to think fast. "Um . . ."

"Can Mr. Nibbles come home with us?" Tess interrupted, flashing Abby a grin.

Mom looked at Tess with a puzzled frown. "Who is Mr. Nibbles?"

"Nobody," said Abby quickly.

"A hamster," said Tess, ignoring Abby. She pulled free of Mom's arms and stepped away. When Tess was excited, she waved her arms when she talked. But before she could say another word, she slipped on a yellow piece of paper and landed in a heap on the floor.

"Oow," Tess howled. She rubbed her elbow. "Who left that dumb paper there?"

It was the permission slip. Abby had to grab it before Mom saw it!

Too late. Mom helped Tess to her feet and reached for the note. "This is from your teacher, Abby," she said, raising an eyebrow.

Abby stared at the floor. She didn't know what to say.

Mom read the note in silence. When she looked at Abby, her eyes were sympathetic. "Please explain," she said gently.

"There's nothing to explain," Abby said defensively. "It's just a big mistake, that's all. Mrs. Hernandez wanted a volunteer to take care of the class pet over spring break."

"Mr. Nibbles is your class pet?" Mom asked.

Abby nodded. "But don't worry. I'll tell her first thing tomorrow that I can't look after him. I should have told her today, after school, except I was kind of embarrassed."

Abby hesitated, staring at the yellow

paper. "But I really wanted to do it," she added softly.

"I'm surprised at you, Abby," Mom said in a reproachful voice.

Abby sighed. Not only did she have to explain to Mrs. Hernandez that she couldn't take Mr. Nibbles, but now Mom was disappointed in her. This wasn't turning out to be such a great day.

"I'm sorry," she said.

"I'm surprised you gave up so easily."

Abby was caught off guard. "Huh?"

Mom put her arm around Abby's shoulders. "You're usually much more persistent."

"But the rule . . ."

"I know the rule. But I also know that the building superintendent is away on vacation for two weeks. His son is looking after things. I think his name is Desmond. Anyway, he likes animals. Maybe you should talk to him."

Abby couldn't believe her ears. Was it true? Would old Mr. Brewster's son let her keep Mr. Nibbles in her bedroom? A thrill of excitement swept through her. Maybe there was hope after all!

"I'm going to talk to him," she cried, heading for the door.

"Oh no you don't," Mom said, still smiling. She pointed at Abby's backpack. "Do your homework first. You can talk to Desmond later."

Abby groaned. "But . . ."

Mom crossed her arms and shook her head. "Homework."

Abby knew there was no point in arguing. She pulled her math binder and pencil case out of her backpack and followed Mom to the kitchen. It didn't matter, really, she thought, dumping her stuff on the table. Nothing mattered now that she might be able to bring Mr. Nibbles home. It would be like having her very own pet!

Tess poked her head into the kitchen and stuck out her tongue at Abby. "I told you to ask Mom."

5 Like Father, Like Son?

Usually Abby loved math, but today her homework seemed to take forever. And when Mom checked it she found four mistakes. With a sigh, Abby picked up her eraser and went back to work.

A few minutes later she handed her binder to Mom for approval. "Can I go talk to Mr. Brewster's son now?" Abby asked impatiently.

"Okay," Mom said when she'd made sure Abby's corrections were right. "Go ahead. And take Tess with you."

"But . . ." Abby protested.

"Take Tess with you," Mom repeated firmly. "She's your helper, right?"

"Yeah, okay," grumbled Abby. She was still annoyed at Tess for being such a blabbermouth. Tess couldn't keep a secret if her life depended on it. Still, Abby had to admit, this time it had worked out pretty well.

Abby peeked into the living room. Tess

was on the floor, playing a game of checkers with herself. She moved a red checker, then scooted around to the opposite side and jumped it with a black one.

"Gotcha!" she said gleefully.

"I'm going to talk to Mr. Brewster's son," Abby said. "Wanna come?"

"Woof!" Tess jumped to her feet, sending the checkerboard and the checkers flying. She hopped over the mess, her game immediately forgotten.

Mr. Brewster's apartment was on the first floor of the building. Whenever anyone needed him they could almost always find him there, sitting in front of the television watching a baseball game. He was an old man with gray hair and bushy eyebrows that crouched above his eyes like two furry caterpillars.

He was grumpy too. He never smiled or waved when he passed Abby and Tess in the hallway. When Mom or Dad called him to come fix something, he always arrived late. He muttered under his breath as he entered their apartment, his dented red toolbox clutched in his hand.

No one had ever told Abby that Mr. Brewster had a son. In fact, Abby realized, she didn't know anything about the superintendent, even though they'd lived in his building for three years. Well, she knew he hated animals.

"I hope Desmond is nicer than his father," Abby said to Tess as they stopped in front of the right door. "I guess he must be if he likes animals."

"Woof," agreed Tess.

Abby hesitated a moment, then knocked twice.

6 Mr. Bumblebee

Nothing happened.

"Maybe he's not home," Tess suggested. "We could come back later."

"We can't," Abby replied. "I've got to return the permission slip to Mrs. Hernandez tomorrow." She rapped her knuckles sharply on the door.

The minutes ticked by. Abby bit her lip. She couldn't walk away now, not when she was so close. Just as she reached out to knock again, the door flew open and a man appeared in the doorway.

Abby couldn't help staring. He wore black

and yellow striped bicycle shorts and a bright yellow T-shirt. His arms bulged with muscles and his short hair stuck straight out from his head in every direction. He reminded Abby of a bumblebee.

"Uh, we're looking for Mr. Brewster's son," Abby said tentatively. She wondered if this strangely dressed man could hear her over the tinny music that blared from the headphones covering his ears. "Do you know where we can find him?"

Mr. Bumblebee flashed a good-natured smile and pressed a button on his Walkman. Instantly the music stopped.

"Sorry, kids," he said with a chuckle. "Couldn't hear you, my tunes were too loud."

Abby tried again. "We're looking for Mr. Brewster's son."

"Well, you found him," he answered cheerfully. "You can call me Desmond."

"You're Desmond?" Abby found it hard to believe that this loud, spiky-haired insect was Mr. Brewster's son. She couldn't imagine the two of them in the same room together, let alone the same family.

He must have caught the doubt in her voice. "That's what they call me," he said with a grin. His eyes crinkled up at the corners. "I'm watching the building while Dad's away. What can I do for you?"

Abby turned to Tess for help, but Tess was speechless. For once Abby wished she would say something. Usually Tess wouldn't stop talking. Trust her to pick a time like this to clam up.

"We were just wondering . . ." Abby started, then stopped. She cleared her throat. "I mean, we wanted to ask you if it would be okay . . ."

Abby and Tess gaped.

Desmond was jumping up and down in the doorway, swinging his arms forward, then back. Suddenly he dropped his head to his chest, then rolled it to one side. "Go on, I'm listening."

"Um, well . . ." Abby watched uncertainly as he switched from jogging on the spot to doing jumping jacks. "Our family lives in number 18. We wondered if you'd let us bring a hamster home from school. It's only for a week," she added quickly, so he wouldn't get the wrong idea. "Just over spring break."

"A hamster?" asked Desmond, bending sideways at the waist and stretching one arm in the air over his head. "In your apartment?"

Abby nodded.

Desmond seemed to be thinking it over. He bent forward and touched the tips of his fingers to his yellow sneakers. Tilting his head, he looked up at them. "Just for a week?" he asked.

Abby nodded again.

"Okay," he said, straightening up. "But listen, kids. You have to promise me that this hamster of yours will stay in your apartment, in its cage. If something goes wrong and my dad finds out about it, then we'll all be in trouble. Got it?"

"Oh, thank you," Abby nearly hugged Desmond. She couldn't believe her luck! "Don't worry," she said, "we'll be extra careful. We're pet-sitters, so we know how to take good care of animals."

"Well, great. Then I don't have to worry about your hamster escaping or anything like that. Because my dad . . ."

"We'll be careful," Abby assured him. She remembered how the lizard they'd taken care of had escaped from his vivarium, but she pushed that thought aside. "We're very responsible."

"Cool. Then it'll be no problem." Desmond hit a button on his Walkman and the music blared from his headphones. He jogged out into the hall and shut the door behind him. "Gotta run, kids. Four miles a day, rain or shine!"

With a wave, he was off. Abby and Tess watched him trot down the hallway and disappear through the front door of the building.

"He's kind of strange," said Abby slowly. "Did you see his shoes?"

Tess giggled.

"Well, I don't care how strange he is," Abby decided, "because thanks to him, Mr. Nibbles is coming home with us tomorrow!"

7 Homeward Bound

Mrs. Hernandez handed Abby a box of hamster food. "Okay, I think that's everything," she said. "Are you sure you know what to do?"

Abby stuffed the box full of seeds and nuts into her backpack. It reminded her of the trail mix Mom sometimes packed in their lunches. "Yes, Mrs. Hernandez. I'll feed Mr. Nibbles every night before I go to bed. I'll also make sure his water bottle is full. And I'll give him a few slices of a fruit or a vegetable every morning. You don't have to worry."

"I'm sure you'll do a wonderful job," Mrs. Hernandez said. "It's very reassuring to know that Mr. Nibbles will be in good hands next week. I know we haven't had him in the class-room that long, but I'm rather attached to the little fellow."

Abby shrugged into her backpack and picked up the cage. It wasn't very heavy, but it was big. When she held it out in front of her, she could just barely see over the top.

"Try not to handle him too much at first," advised Mrs. Hernandez as Abby headed out the door. "He'll be nervous in a new environment. Give him a day or two to settle in."

"I will," called Abby over her shoulder. The weight of the cage shifted as Mr. Nibbles moved from one end to the other. Abby walked as carefully as she could, concentrating on keeping it steady.

Tess was waiting for her outside. "Is that Mr. Nibbles?" she panted, jumping up and down with excitement.

"Don't bump me, Tess," Abby warned.

"Do you want me to carry your backpack?" Tess asked hopefully. Abby could see she was eager to help.

"It's okay. Let's just go." Abby's arms were beginning to ache and they weren't even out of the schoolyard yet. "The sooner he gets settled in our bedroom, the better."

Tess skipped along beside Abby. She walked as quickly as she dared. Every now and then a tiny squeak could be heard from the pile of bedding Mr. Nibbles had burrowed into. Abby hoped he wasn't getting seasick. Finally she could see their big brown apartment building up ahead.

"Hold on, Mr. Nibbles," she whispered softly. "We're almost there."

As they got closer Tess spotted Mom sitting on the front steps. She yelped with delight and raced ahead. Abby continued to walk with the cage balanced carefully in front of her. By the time she reached their building, Tess had clambered onto Mom's lap and was happily nuzzling her neck.

"This must be the wonderful Mr. Nibbles I've heard so much about," Mom said as soon as Abby was within earshot.

Abby smiled wearily. She was slightly out of breath from the walk. Lugging the cage home had turned out to be harder than she'd expected. Gently, she set it on the step beside Mom and then flopped down beside it.

Mom looked at Mr. Nibbles, who'd poked

his head out of the bedding. “He’s kind of cute, isn’t he? Just like a little stuffed animal.”

“He’s a teddy bear hamster,” said Abby proudly. She sat up straighter and added, “Actually, he’s a Syrian hamster, but lots of people call them teddy bear hamsters because they’re long-haired and furry. Mrs. Hernandez taught us all about them when we got him.”

Mom watched Mr. Nibbles twitch his nose. “How old is he?”

Abby looked at the cage doubtfully. “I don’t know, exactly. We only got him two weeks ago.”

Tess crawled off Mom’s lap to investigate. She sniffed the cage inquisitively. Suddenly she yipped and jumped back, wrinkling her nose in distaste.

“He stinks,” she declared.

8 A New Roommate

"Hamsters don't stink," Abby said, throwing Tess a dirty look. "For your information, they have almost no body odor at all. It's the cage that smells, and that's because it needs to be cleaned. I'll clean it out tomorrow, after he settles in."

Mom stood and picked up Abby's backpack. "I'll carry this inside," she said. "We need to figure out where we're going to put Mr. Nibbles."

"I thought we'd set him up on the dresser in our bedroom," said Abby.

"But aren't hamsters nocturnal?" asked Mom doubtfully. "He might keep you awake at night."

Abby knew that nocturnal meant Mr. Nibbles was an animal that slept during the day and was active at night. It was true that at school he spent most of his time curled up in a ball, fast asleep. But if they were only allowed to have a pet for one week, she wanted to spend as much time with it as possible.

"He won't," Abby promised. "If I can sleep through the opera music from the apartment below, a little hamster won't keep me awake." Abby didn't care how much noise Mr. Nibbles made. This was her one chance to have a pet and she wasn't going to miss a minute of it.

Up in the apartment they headed straight to the bedroom. On Abby's side of the room there was a bed, a desk and a bookshelf full of animal books. Tess's bed was on the opposite side, next to an overflowing toy box and a low, wide dresser.

Abby set the cage on the dresser. She'd rather have Mr. Nibbles on her side of the room, but the dresser was bigger than the desk. She needed the extra space for Mr. Nibbles' food and the wood shavings that lined the bottom of his cage.

Tess stood in the doorway, watching. "Can I help?" she asked.

Abby pulled Mr. Nibbles' water bottle

from her bag. It was made of clear plastic and had a metal spout poking out the bottom. A small ball blocked the spout, keeping the water inside until the hamster licked it. With every lick, Mr. Nibbles got a tiny droplet of water.

"Here," Abby said to Tess. "Go fill this up, okay? It has to be filled with fresh water every day. That can be your job."

Tess yipped happily. She grabbed the plastic bottle and raced off to the bathroom.

The sound of running water burbled across the hall.

Abby grinned. Being in charge of the water bottle was the perfect job for Tess. It was completely foolproof. The bottle clipped onto the outside of the wire cage, which meant Tess would never have to unlatch the door.

Abby rearranged the hamster supplies, congratulating herself on thinking of the perfect way to keep Tess out of trouble. This was one pet-sitting job where nothing was going to go wrong.

9 Tess Makes a Friend

"Can I hold him?" pleaded Tess.

"I already told you no," said Abby. "Stop bugging me."

Tess gazed at Abby with puppy-dog eyes. "Just for a minute?"

Abby shook her head. "Mrs. Hernandez said not to handle him right away. You have to let him get used to a strange place, you know. He's an animal, not a toy."

"Please?"

Abby sighed and dropped the book she was reading onto her pillow. It was obvious Tess wasn't going to let up. She hadn't given Abby a moment's peace since they'd finished supper an hour ago. *The Complete Guide to Hamsters* would have to wait until later.

"If I let you pet him, will you promise to leave me alone for awhile?"

Tess grinned. "Woof!"

The wire cage sat squarely on top of the

dresser. Mr. Nibbles was curled up in a corner, sleeping peacefully. Abby and Tess watched him for a minute, hoping he'd wake up.

"Wow," breathed Tess. "He's fat!"

"He's not fat, he's just furry," corrected Abby. "Teddy bear hamsters have longer fur than some of the other kinds."

Tess peered closer. "I think he's fat."

Abby didn't argue. Tess could be stubborn when she wanted to be.

"What's that round thing?" asked Tess, pointing to a plastic contraption hooked to the bars on one end of the cage.

"It's an exercise wheel," Abby explained. "It spins around when Mr. Nibbles runs in it. It's kind of like a treadmill in a gym."

"He should use it more," said Tess. "He's way too fat."

"I told you, he's not fat," Abby began, exasperated. Then she stopped. Why should she care what Tess thought? It was easier to just change the subject. "I think it's time to feed him. Pass me that box, would you?"

Sunflower seeds, peanuts, corn and a bunch of other things could be seen through the clear plastic lid. Tess sniffed the box before handing it to Abby.

"Yummy," she said. "Can I try some?"

"Don't be gross, Tess." Abby picked up the box and scanned the long list of ingredients. "Do you really want to eat rodent pellets? And flaked peas and barley . . . and dog biscuits?"

Tess cocked her head to one side and thought for a moment.

"Forget I asked," said Abby. She wouldn't put it past Tess to say yes. Especially if the mixture contained dog biscuits. "It's for Mr. Nibbles, so hands off, understand?"

Tess nodded reluctantly. Abby opened the door to the cage and reached inside. Just as she was about to pick up the food dish, Mr. Nibbles uncurled himself and stood up. When he saw Abby's hand, he backed away quickly.

"He doesn't like you," whispered Tess, watching the hamster intently.

Abby laughed. "What are you talking

about? I feed him at school all the time. He's just confused. I told you it would be awhile before he got used to a new room."

Mr. Nibbles took a few more steps backwards. Abby hesitated. What was he doing? There was something different about the way he was staring at her. He almost looked angry. Taking a deep breath, she reached for the dish again.

Mr. Nibbles darted forward and made a strange grating noise. Abby yanked her hand back in surprise. He was really mad at her! Her hand shook a little as she closed the door and latched it.

Could Tess be right? Abby stared at Mr. Nibbles. The grating noise had stopped, but he was still looking at her in an aggressive way. Determined not to be afraid, Abby unlatched the cage door and put her hand inside. Immediately the noise started up again. She pulled her hand back. The noise stopped.

"He doesn't like you," repeated Tess.

Abby frowned. "I don't get it," she said,

frustrated. "I've never seen him act like this before."

"Let me try," suggested Tess.

"If he doesn't want me near him, he's not going to let you near him," Abby said confidently. "Maybe he needs more time . . ."

Without waiting for Abby to finish her sentence, Tess reached inside for the food dish. Mr. Nibbles eyed her, his nose twitching, but he remained silent as she picked it up. Tess handed the dish to Abby.

“I don’t understand,” exclaimed Abby. “Why did he let you get the dish?”

“We’re friends,” Tess said simply.

“Don’t be ridiculous,” Abby snapped. Scowling, she filled the dish with hamster food and handed it to Tess. “Put it in quickly so he doesn’t bite you.”

“He won’t,” Tess said. She replaced the food dish and patted Mr. Nibbles’ furry back. “See?”

Abby bit her lip and turned away. It wasn’t fair! Mr. Nibbles was *her* class pet. Not Tess’s. Why did he let Tess pet him and not her? She finally got a chance to have a pet, and the stupid thing didn’t even like her!

What good was a pet you couldn’t even touch?

10 A Present for Mr. Nibbles

Tess fed Mr. Nibbles the next day. And the day after that. Abby also let her put fresh wood chips on the floor of his cage. In fact, she let Tess do everything.

It wasn't that Abby didn't want to take care of Mr. Nibbles. She did. But every time she tried to get close to him, he acted funny. He made that grating noise with his teeth and scurried away with an indignant squeak. As much as Abby hated to admit it, Tess was right. Mr. Nibbles liked Tess, but he didn't like Abby.

It was as if he were a completely different hamster from the class pet Abby knew at school. For one thing, he seemed to eat a lot more. He ate everything Tess gave him and still acted hungry. He'd stand by his food dish and stare at Tess, waiting for a second helping. Abby didn't remember him being so greedy at school.

"Some pet you are," she muttered, glancing up from the book she was reading on her bed. The fluffy ball asleep in one corner of the cage didn't respond. Abby turned a few pages of her book in silence. It was about kittens. She had stuck *The Complete Guide to Hamsters* in the very bottom of her bookshelf, as far away from her bed as possible.

When the doorbell rang Abby jumped up and raced down the hall. Tess was over at a friend's house for the afternoon. It wasn't often that Abby got the bedroom all to herself, so she had called Rachel right away.

"Hi Abby," said Rachel when Abby opened the door. "I brought a surprise."

Abby looked at the plastic shopping bag in Rachel's hand. It was big and round, as if it held a bowling ball. But that didn't make sense because Rachel hated bowling. She said it was because the rental shoes were gross, but Abby didn't believe her. Rachel probably didn't like bowling because she was terrible at it.

"What kind of surprise?" Abby asked.

Rachel hid the bag behind her back. "I'll show you in a minute. Where's Mr. Nibbles?"

"He's in my room," said Abby without enthusiasm. "Do you want to bake some cookies?"

"Maybe later," Rachel said. "First I want to see Mr. Nibbles. The surprise is for him."

Abby followed her to the bedroom. "He's been acting kind of strange ever since I brought him home," she warned Rachel. "I don't know if he'll let you touch him."

Rachel glanced over her shoulder. "What do you mean, strange?"

Abby shrugged. "I don't know. Moody, I guess. He won't let me near him, but all of a sudden Tess is his best friend."

"Weird," said Rachel. "Where is Tess, anyway? She'd like to see this too."

"At a friend's," answered Abby. She flopped down on her bed, ignoring the hamster cage.

"Wow, I've never seen this room so clean," said Rachel, looking around. Abby was a neat freak. She kept her half of the room tidy and organized. Tess, on the other hand, had a tendency to toss her toys and clothes all over the place.

"Mom made Tess pick up her stuff before she could go out," Abby said. "It's amazing how fast she can clean up when she wants to." She glanced at Rachel's bag. "So what's the big surprise?"

Rachel smiled secretively and turned her back to Abby. The bag rustled as she pulled something out of it. With a flourish, she turned around. "Ta-dah!"

Abby immediately recognized the surprise. "Hey, I know what that is. It's an exercise ball," she exclaimed, jumping up and taking it from Rachel. "Jeremy has a bunch of them down at the pet store."

A few weeks ago Jeremy had let Abby take one out of its box. She had decided right then and there that if she ever got a hamster, she'd buy it an exercise ball. Maybe a blue one. They came in all sorts of fun colors.

This one was the same size as a bowling ball, the big kind with holes for your fingers. It was made of clear yellow plastic and was hollow in the middle. There was a trap door on one side for the hamster to go in and out. Once inside, the hamster could make the ball roll across the floor just by walking or running.

"My big brother used to have a hamster. We still have all the equipment and stuff. I thought Mr. Nibbles might like to play in it."

"Cool," Abby said. She forgot for a minute

that she was miffed at Mr. Nibbles. "He can explore the whole room. It's perfect! He won't be able to get lost or hurt or stepped on."

"He won't be able to leave a trail of poop everywhere he goes, either," said Rachel with a grin. "Try it."

"Okay," Abby said uncertainly, looking over at Mr. Nibbles. He was awake for once, nibbling on a carrot stick Tess had given him earlier. "I hope he'll let me pick him up."

Nervously she unlatched the cage door and reached inside. But it happened again. As soon as her hand got near Mr. Nibbles, he skittered away and ground his teeth at her.

Abby quickly pulled her hand back and frowned. "We'll have to wait until Tess gets home," she said.

"I've never seen him do that," Rachel said, surprised. "Listen, maybe we should forget it. I can't stay long, and I didn't actually ask my brother if I could borrow the ball."

"Dumb pet," Abby grumbled. Nothing was working out the way she wanted.

11 Someone Is Forgotten

Rachel looked at Abby's crestfallen face, then at Mr. Nibbles. "I've got an idea," she said. She picked up the box of hamster food. "Is this what he eats?"

"Uh huh," said Abby slowly. "It's got dog biscuits in it, so don't get any funny ideas."

"I'm not going to eat it," Rachel grimaced. She opened the ball and dropped a bit of hamster food inside. The she held the open door of the ball against the opening to the cage.

The girls waited. After a minute Mr. Nibbles stepped up to the cage door, sniffing curiously. Abby and Rachel held their breath. Mr. Nibbles hesitated, but the scent of the food was too tempting and finally he climbed into the ball.

Rachel quickly closed the trap door. "I did it," she smiled triumphantly at Abby. "Hey, what's that thing around his neck?"

"A bracelet," Abby answered, glancing at

the greenish-white ring. "Tess pretends it's her flea collar, but since it's too small for her, she put it on Mr. Nibbles. It looks silly, I know, but he won't let me take it off."

Rachel set the ball gently on the carpet. For a moment nothing happened. Then Mr. Nibbles took a step forward, then another, and soon the ball was rolling across the room.

Rachel laughed out loud when the ball bumped into the wall. "He needs driving lessons," she joked.

"He'll figure it out," said Abby. She watched Mr. Nibbles change directions and roll into the middle of the room. He looked like he was having fun. She could imagine how boring it must be to be cooped up in a small cage day after day.

Back and forth he went, enjoying his new freedom. He explored the room, rolling under Abby's bed, then under her desk. Rachel had to rescue him once when he rolled into a corner and got stuck.

"Come on," Abby said finally, growing

impatient. For someone who didn't like hamsters, Rachel was sure having a lot of fun with Mr. Nibbles. "He'll be safe in here. Let's go bake some cookies."

"Only if they're double chocolate chip," Rachel said, following Abby out the door. They laughed and talked as they walked down the long hallway to the kitchen.

Abby was just pulling the last batch of cookies from the oven when Tess got home. She walked into the kitchen, sniffing loudly.

"Mmmmm . . . chocolate chip cookies!" Tess's nose led her directly to the cookies cooling on the table. "Can I have one?"

Abby and Rachel grinned at each other. They'd lost count of how many cookies they'd already devoured. Abby had even burnt her tongue trying to eat one still hot from the oven. Mom would disapprove if she knew, but she'd been in her studio all afternoon, hard at work on a painting.

"Sure, help yourself," Abby said. "We were just going to make a plate to bring to Mom."

Tess stuffed two cookies in her mouth and ran ahead of Abby and Rachel. “I’m home,” she yelled, barking cheerfully and flinging the studio door open.

The older girls followed behind slowly. By the time they got to the studio, Tess was busy helping Mom clean her paintbrushes.

“We did some baking,” Abby said, balancing a tray of cookies and juice in front of her.

“Hi girls,” said Mom. “I thought I smelled something delicious.”

“Me too,” giggled Tess. She gave the air

another sniff.

Mom laughed. "Did you have fun at Miki's house?"

Tess panted happily. "We played circus and had a parade and dressed up and ate carrots and apples and watched cartoons and . . ."

"Try one," Abby interrupted, holding out the plate to Mom. Tess could ramble on and on forever. "While they're still warm."

Mom bit into a cookie and brushed a crumb from her lip. "Delectable, as usual," she said with a smile. "I always enjoy it when you and Rachel bake."

"Me too," said Rachel. "But I have to go now." She looked at Abby. "I need my ball."

"You played ball?" asked Tess. "I want to play too."

"It's not that kind of a ball," Abby explained. "It's an exercise ball for Mr. Nibbles. He's in it right now, rolling around in the bedroom."

"Woof," barked Tess excitedly. "I want to see!"

They left the cookies with Mom and went to the bedroom. Tess raced ahead again. Abby and Rachel were almost there when they heard a terrible sound. Alarmed, they ran the last few steps. Tess stood beside the empty hamster cage, howling.

"What's wrong?" demanded Abby.

"He's gone," wailed Tess. "You lost Mr. Nibbles!"

Abby sighed. "Stop making that awful noise, Tess. Mr. Nibbles isn't lost. I told you, he's in Rachel's exercise ball."

"You promised you'd take care of him while I was at Miki's," cried Tess. "I told you he wasn't feeling good today."

"I did take care of him," Abby retorted. "Mr. Nibbles is just fine. He really likes the exercise ball. And he can't get lost in it. It's absolutely impossible."

Tess stopped howling. She looked around the room tearfully. "Then where is he?"

12 Hide and Seek

Good question, thought Abby. Where was Mr. Nibbles? She looked around the room, but the round plastic ball was nowhere to be seen. She glanced at Rachel, who shrugged.

"Well," said Abby, searching for an explanation. "He must have rolled out of sight, that's all. We'll just have to look for him. But," she added quickly, before Tess could start howling again, "he's definitely not lost."

Tess wiped her nose on her sleeve. "He's hiding?"

"Sure," Rachel jumped in. "Hide and seek. He found a hiding spot and we're supposed to look for him."

Tess brightened at this. "A game?"

"That's right," said Abby. "Want to play? The first person who finds him, wins."

"I'm going to win," Tess said, happy once again, "because I'm going to use my super sense of smell, just like I did with the cookies."

But Mr. Nibbles had disappeared. Not even Tess, tiptoeing around with her nose in the air, could find him. They looked under the bed, behind the toy box, beneath the desk and behind the bedroom door.

No hamster.

Abby checked in the closet, but all she saw was a mound of dirty clothes. So that's how Tess cleaned up so quickly, she thought. She should have known. Tess never put her dirty clothes in the hamper. It was as if she were allergic to laundry or something.

She turned back to the room. In spite of her reassuring words to Tess, she was beginning to feel concerned.

"Tess, was the bedroom door shut before you came in here?" she asked.

Tess thought about it for a minute. Then she shook her head. "Nope."

Abby and Rachel exchanged glances. "Maybe we'd better search the whole apartment," said Abby.

They scoured the apartment looking for Mr. Nibbles. Abby went to her parents' bedroom while Rachel searched the kitchen. The two of them spent ten minutes in the living room, checking every possible hiding place. They rummaged through the front hall closet. Abby even opened the front door of the apartment and looked outside.

Tess, still following her nose, checked in the refrigerator, under the doormat and in the bathtub.

Still no hamster.

"I've really got to go," Rachel said finally. "I'll have to pick up the exercise ball later, I guess."

"Sorry," Abby said. "I'll find it for you. Don't worry." She tried to smile confidently as she shut the front door behind Rachel.

Abby and Tess searched the apartment a second time. When they were done, Tess looked at Abby with tears in her eyes.

"He's lost now, isn't he?"

"Well, kind of," admitted Abby. "But it's more like he's misplaced. He's here somewhere, we just have to find him. Too bad you can't whistle for him like you would for a puppy."

Tess rubbed her eyes. She looked like she was going to cry again. "I knew he wasn't feeling good today."

"Mr. Nibbles is perfectly healthy," Abby assured her. "I don't know why you keep saying he isn't."

"He's sick. I can tell," said Tess tearfully.

"I should have stayed home."

Abby patted her arm. "It's not your fault, Tess."

"I know," said Tess. She glared at Abby. "It's your fault. And Rachel's."

Abby opened her mouth to protest, then closed it again. Tess had a point. She shouldn't have left Mr. Nibbles unsupervised, even if he *was* in an exercise ball. But Rachel had been paying too much attention to him. She'd come over to play with Abby, after all, not the hamster.

"Look," said Abby. "He's not in any danger. He can't get hurt. He'll just sit where he is until we find him. There's nothing to get upset about."

Suddenly she had an awful thought. What if the trap door had somehow popped open? If that had happened, Mr. Nibbles could be anywhere!

"But he's lost," cried Tess, her eyes growing even wider. "And scared and sick. Poor Mr. Nibbles!"

"I told you, he's not sick . . ." began Abby.

But Tess didn't want to listen. She threw her head back and howled. The mournful sound bounced off the walls and brought Mom running.

"What's going on?" she cried.

"Abby lost Mr. Nibbles," wailed Tess. "He's gone forever!"

Mom looked at Abby. "Is it true?"

Abby bit her lip. "Well, not really. I mean, he's not gone forever. He's in the apartment somewhere. We just have to find him."

Mom glanced at the cage. "He escaped?"

"Not exactly," said Abby slowly. "I kind of, um, let him go."

13 A Ghostly Green Glow

"He's not running around free or anything," Abby hurried to explain. "He's in Rachel's exercise ball. He can't get out and nothing can hurt him." She tried not to imagine the trap door springing open.

Mom raised one eyebrow. "So where is he now?"

Abby squirmed under Mom's gaze. "Well, that's the problem. Rachel and I kind of left him alone while we baked cookies. I didn't think he'd go far."

"I see," said Mom. She didn't say anything else, but Abby knew what she was thinking. A responsible pet-sitter wouldn't put a hamster in a ball and then go bake cookies. Abby tried to think quickly.

"Hamsters are nocturnal, right? So he's probably sleeping somewhere. He'll wake up pretty soon and start rolling around, looking for food. We'll hear the noise and find him. No problem." Abby hoped she sounded convincing.

"Poor, hungry Mr. Nibbles," sniffled Tess. She buried her head in Mom's shoulder.

"I hope you're right, Abby," Mom said, her arms around Tess. "Because you made Desmond Brewster a promise."

Abby swallowed hard. She had sworn to Desmond that Mr. Nibbles wouldn't escape. And he hadn't, not really. He was just . . . misplaced.

With Mom's help they went through the apartment again. Dad came home from work in time to help them move the sofa in the living room to look behind it. He even pulled the TV stand out of the corner so Tess could check if the ball was caught in the wires and cables. They didn't find Mr. Nibbles.

Finally Mom decided it was time to make supper. They had a silent meal that night. Tess picked at her food, using the back of her hand every now and then to wipe away a tear. Abby felt awful.

As they brushed their teeth before getting

into bed, Abby tried to reason with Tess.

"He's not gone," she said for the tenth time, wishing she believed her own words. "We'll find him. I promise."

"You promised the bumblebee man that Mr. Nibbles wouldn't get lost," Tess accused her. "I don't believe you anymore."

"He's perfectly safe," Abby said, exasperated. Tess acted like she was the only one who cared about Mr. Nibbles. Didn't she realize that Abby felt bad too?

But Tess refused to listen. She raced out of the bathroom and Abby heard their closet door slam shut with a bang. Abby groaned. Tess always hid in the bedroom closet when she was upset.

Abby followed Tess slowly. She hesitated in the hallway, trying to decide between her bedroom and the studio. Should she go talk to Mom? It would feel so good to tell everything to someone. But right now Tess needed comfort too. This whole mess was Abby's fault, after all. She entered the bedroom.

"Tess?" she called through the closet door.

"Go away."

"I want to talk to you," Abby said. "Please?"

Tess hiccuped. "I'm not coming out."

Abby thought for a moment. "Can I come in then?"

There was a pause, then a tiny, "Okay."

Abby pulled the door partway open and stepped into the dark space. There was barely room to move. The closet stored board games and stuffed animals and an old doll stroller. On top of that was stuff Tess had thrown in so the bedroom would look tidy. And just inside the door was Tess's dirty laundry.

Abby stepped over the mound of clothes and cleared a spot beside Tess. They sat side by side, their shoulders touching. The closet was barely wide enough for the metal hangers that held their shirts and dresses.

"It's kind of messy in here," Abby said. She could just make out the lines of Tess's face. She was staring straight ahead.

Tess folded her arms over her chest. "You forgot to close the door," she said stiffly.

"Sorry." Abby stood up and climbed back over the pile of laundry. She grabbed the doorknob and pulled the door shut. Instantly the closet was pitched into darkness. Holding her hands in front of her face like a shield, Abby stumbled her way back to Tess.

"We'll find Mr. Nibbles, you know," she said, trying to keep the irritation out of her voice.

"We will?" Tess whispered.

Abby nodded, then she realized Tess

couldn't see her. "I promise. And I mean it this time."

"But you don't even like Mr. Nibbles. I think you let him get lost on purpose."

Abby thought for a moment. "It's not that I don't like him," she tried to explain. "He doesn't like me. He won't let me near him. I guess that hurt my feelings, you know? But I didn't lose him on purpose. I wouldn't do that."

"Really?"

"Really," said Abby firmly. "We'll look for him again first thing in the morning. Don't worry, okay?"

Just as she tried to stand up, Tess clutched at her arm. Abby sat back down abruptly. "Hey, that hurts . . ."

"Shhh," hissed Tess in her ear. "Look!"

Abby scanned the inside of the closet, but all she could see was black. Then her eye caught a flicker low to the floor a few feet in front of her. It was a ghostly green glow.

Abby blinked. It flickered again. Then it was gone.

14 An Amazing Discovery

"What was that?" asked Tess in a shaky whisper.

Abby had no idea. It made no sense. What could possibly be glowing in their bedroom closet? Her heart thudded in her chest.

The strange light shone again, so faint that Abby wondered if her eyes were playing tricks on her. It reminded Abby of something she'd seen before, but she couldn't quite figure out what.

"I'm scared," whimpered Tess. She tightened her grip on Abby's arm.

Abby was a little scared too, but she

didn't want Tess to know. "I'm sure it's nothing," she said loudly. "Look, I'll prove it to you."

Acting braver than she felt, Abby crawled toward the dirty clothes, her eyes fixed on the spot where she'd seen the mysterious light.

It was gone.

She stood up and threw open the door. Light from the bedroom streamed into the closet. "See," she said, secretly relieved. "There's nothing there."

"But . . ." Tess wasn't convinced.

Abby knelt down near the spot where they'd seen the strange glow. Now that the closet was full of light, it felt foolish to be frightened. She tossed unwashed socks and crumpled blue jeans onto the bedroom floor.

"I'm telling you," she said, "there's nothing here. It must have been a reflection or an optical illusion or . . ."

She stopped mid-sentence.

"What is it?" asked Tess, her voice squeaking with fear.

"I don't believe it," cried Abby softly. She

looked at Tess, a strange expression on her face. "You've got to see this."

Tess refused to move. "Is it a ghost?"

Abby shook her head. "Nope. Not even close. I've found Mr. Nibbles. And that's not all."

"Mr. Nibbles?" Tess crept forward. "You found him? But the glow . . ."

"You're not going to believe this," said Abby. "Not in a million years."

Crowding close to Abby for safety, Tess peered cautiously into the pile of laundry.

Rachel's round exercise ball was half covered by a wrinkled blue sweater and Tess's favorite T-shirt turned inside out. Inside the ball was Mr. Nibbles. He stared up at Abby and Tess through the clear plastic, the flea collar around his neck no longer glowing. Curled up around him were a bunch of tiny, wriggling pink bodies.

Mr. Nibbles had given birth!

15 The More the Merrier

"Babies!" cried Tess.

"Puppies," corrected Abby in a breathless voice. "Hamster babies are called puppies. I read about them in my book."

Tess looked confused. "Isn't that impossible? Mr. Nibbles is a . . ."

"Female," finished Abby. A slow grin spread across her face. "Mr. Nibbles must really be Mrs. Nibbles!"

Tess inched closer, but Abby held her back. "Careful, Tess. We can't disturb them or Mr. Nibbles, I mean, Mrs. Nibbles, might reject them."

Tess looked puzzled.

"When hamster puppies get touched by humans, sometimes their mother doesn't want them anymore," Abby explained. "It's got something to do with their smell, I think. We'd better tell Mom and Dad."

They found their parents relaxing in front

of the television.

"Mr. Nibbles is a mommy," exclaimed Tess, throwing herself at Mom. She barked happily. "He has babies!"

Mom looked baffled. "What?"

Abby grinned and nodded. "It's true. We've got a whole bunch of puppies in our bedroom closet."

"Puppies? In your closet?" Dad sounded stunned.

Abby and Tess dragged their parents down the hall. "You've got to see this for yourselves," Abby said with a laugh.

Mom drew in a sharp breath when she saw the exercise ball full of baby hamsters. "This is unexpected," she said, glancing quickly at Dad.

"Well, I'll be," said Dad, kneeling to get a better look. "What are we going to do with them?"

"They can live in the closet," suggested Tess cheerfully. "I can throw my dirty clothes under my bed instead."

Mom raised an eyebrow. "Interesting idea, Tess. But they can't stay in the closet. And we do have a laundry hamper in the bathroom, you know."

"Yeah," Abby told Tess. "If you weren't such a slob the exercise ball wouldn't have gotten stuck in your clothes."

"The puppies would still have been born," Mom sighed. She turned to Abby and asked, "How long before we can touch them?"

Abby ran to her bookshelf and pulled *The Complete Guide to Hamsters* out from the bottom shelf. "I read about that," she said, flipping through the pages. "Here it is. It says the puppies must not be disturbed for two weeks or the mother may reject them."

"Two weeks," whooped Tess. She raced

around the room in a canine frenzy. "Hooray! Hooray!"

"Tess, sit," ordered Mom.

Tess obediently sat on the edge of her bed. She stared at Mom, panting hopefully.

"We can't keep Mr. Nibbles . . . or whatever her name is, in the closet for two weeks. Anyway, Mr. Brewster will be home from his holidays before then."

Abby had an idea. "Why don't we leave them in the exercise ball?"

Dad shook his head. "Your mom just said they can't stay in the closet, Abby. It's . . ."

"No, wait," interrupted Abby. "What I mean is, why don't we put the exercise ball into the cage? All we have to do is lift the wire top off the base and set it inside. Then we can put the top back on and open the trap door so Mrs. Nibbles can get in and out of the ball to eat and stuff. We won't even have to touch the puppies, and I can take them to school after spring break when I return Mrs. Nibbles. It's perfect!"

Mom smiled. "Let's give it a try."

Together, Abby and Tess unhooked the exercise wheel from the bars of the cage. Now the cage was just wide enough to hold the ball.

Throwing a pointed look in Tess's direction, Mom picked up the dirty clothes around the ball. Tess grinned sheepishly.

Dad cupped the exercise ball in his hands and raised it off the floor, careful not to jostle the newborns. Holding it steady, he carried it across the room and placed it squarely in the center of the bottom of the cage.

After lowering the wire top into place, Abby reached inside the cage and unsnapped the trap door. Now Mrs. Nibbles could get in and out.

Everyone stepped back to watch what would happen.

Mrs. Nibbles crept up to the doorway and sniffed the edges. Abby and Tess held their breath. Would their scent upset her? She sniffed some more, then seemed to make up her mind.

She scampered into the cage and picked up a single wood shaving. Carrying it in her mouth, she returned to her puppies. Abby counted them. One, two, three . . . there were eight of them! They squirmed close to their mother, eager for her warmth.

Abby heaved a sigh of relief. The new mother was nesting. It was going to be okay. It seemed like Mrs. Nibbles didn't mind being moved out of the closet. Of course, Rachel wouldn't be getting the exercise ball back anytime soon, but she'd understand once Abby explained the situation. And what would Mrs. Hernandez and the class think when she came back to school next week with a cage full of hamsters?

Abby grinned at the thought. Instead of taking care of one pet for the week, now she had a whole family of pets. It was the best spring break ever.

"And I just thought Mr. Nibbles was furry," she said with a laugh.

16 Back to School

Abby thought the hamster puppies were ugly. Their little pink bodies were hairless and wrinkly. Their skin was so thin she could see their veins. And they were blind, with eyes that were nothing more than dark spots beneath the skin.

But over spring break the puppies grew and changed.

Five days after they were born they started to grow fur. By Sunday they had begun to blindly explore the interior of the exercise ball, their eyes still firmly shut. Since they were able to move about, Abby decided it was time to take the ball out of the cage.

“Mrs. Nibbles likes you again,” Tess observed.

“I'm glad,” said Abby. Mrs. Nibbles hadn't ground her teeth or squeaked at Abby once since the puppies were born. Her crankiness had disappeared.

Abby removed the wire top of the cage and set it aside. She gently turned the exercise ball until the puppies and their mother slid out the trap door into a soft pile of wood chips. Wrinkling her nose, she set the ball on the floor. After being home to nine hamsters, it needed a good scrubbing.

Working fast, Abby clipped the top of the cage back into place.

"You know, Tess," she said when she was done, "my book says Mrs. Nibbles' strange behavior was pretty normal. When a hamster is pregnant it can become moody and territorial. I just thought she hated me. How was I supposed to know she was pregnant?"

"I knew," Tess said.

"You did not," Abby protested. "Nobody did, not even Mrs. Hernandez."

Tess scratched her ear. "Well, maybe I didn't know she was going to have babies. But I knew she wasn't feeling good. I told you that."

Abby stared at her. "Yeah, right."

"It's true," cried Tess, giving the empty

exercise ball a swift kick. "Why don't you ever listen to me?"

Tess's anger surprised Abby. Why was she so upset? She even had tears in her eyes. "What are you talking about? I listen to you."

Tess flung herself face down on her bed. "You do not," she sobbed into her pillow. "You think I'm a dumb little baby and you never listen to what I say."

"I do so," said Abby. "Don't be ridiculous."

"See?" wailed Tess.

Abby stared at her sister. Was Tess right? Had she been so wrapped up in her own world lately that she hadn't paid attention to what Tess was saying? She thought back over the last week.

She remembered how distraught Tess had been the day Mrs. Nibbles went missing. She had said something about the hamster being sick. But Abby had ignored her. She'd also wanted Abby to show the permission slip to Mom, but she'd ignored that too. How many other times had she dismissed Tess's ideas?

Abby sat down on the bed. Tentatively she put her hand on Tess's shoulder. "I'm sorry," she said quietly. "I guess I haven't been paying attention to you the way I should. Sometimes I forget that you have good ideas. Maybe it's because you're younger than I am . . ."

Tess raised her head from the pillow. "I'm little, but I'm not dumb!"

Abby patted Tess's back the way Dad

sometimes did when they weren't feeling well. "I know. You're not dumb at all. I mean, you were the one who put that glow-in-the-dark flea collar on Mrs. Nibbles. Without it, who knows how long it would have been before we found her? She could have been lost for days!"

Tess sniffed and sat up. "That was pretty smart, wasn't it?"

"Sure it was," said Abby. "In fact, I'd say your flea collar saved the day."

"Yeah, it did," said Tess, happy once again. She wiped away her tears and hopped off the bed. "I'm going to get Mrs. Nibbles a piece of carrot."

Abby listened to her run down the hallway, singing a tuneless song. She was always amazed at how quickly Tess got over her sorrows. A few words of apology or a hug and her hurt feelings vanished. This time Abby had to admit that Tess had good reason to be upset.

On Monday morning it was time to take Mrs. Nibbles and her family back to school. The puppies had grown much stronger in the last seven days and Abby was certain they wouldn't mind the trip. To make sure they'd stay warm and protected, she wrapped an old towel around the cage and secured it with a large safety pin.

On the walk to school Tess trudged along beside Abby. She stared at the sidewalk, her shoulders slumped. Abby glanced at her and laughed quietly to herself. Abby was going to miss the hamsters too, but last night she'd had an idea. A wonderful idea. She couldn't wait to get to school and try it out.

When the morning bell rang Abby waved goodbye to Tess and carried the cage into the classroom. She was careful to keep the towel on.

Her class was in for a surprise!

17 A Brilliant Idea

"Welcome back, class," said Mrs. Hernandez cheerily, walking over to her desk. She did a quick head count and marked her attendance sheet with a pen. "I'm glad to see you're all here today. I hope everyone enjoyed their week off."

The classroom filled with chatter and laughter as everyone talked at once about the fun they'd had over spring break. Abby listened to the noise around her but was too excited to join in. She tapped her foot impatiently. Was the class ever going to get started?

"Settle down, please," Mrs. Hernandez finally said. "You can tell me all about your holiday a little later. Right now I'd like to ask our resident pet-sitter how Mr. Nibbles fared in his new environment. Abby?"

Abby took a deep breath. This was going to be fun. She stood up and carried the cage to her teacher's desk. Setting it down gently, she turned to face the class.

"First of all," she said, trying to look serious, "I'd just like to say that I don't have a hamster in this cage."

"I'll bet she lost him!" shouted Dirk from the back row.

Mrs. Hernandez shot a warning look at Dirk and his friends, then turned to Abby. "Did something happen to Mr. Nibbles?" she asked with a frown.

Abby had trouble keeping a straight face. "Yes," she said solemnly. "I'm afraid so."

There were gasps from the class.

"I don't have a hamster in this cage," repeated Abby, enjoying the drama of the moment. "I have nine."

This time the gasps were louder.

"Nine?" cried Dirk's best friend, Zachary. "What's this, a magic show?"

"That's enough, Zachary," said Mrs. Hernandez. "Abby, please explain."

Reveling in the moment, Abby unpinned the towel and dramatically pulled it away.

"Oh, my," Mrs. Hernandez said weakly.

12
× 4
48

“Mr. Nibbles is a female,” Abby blurted out. “And she had eight puppies last week. They’re kind of cute now, but you should have seen them when they were born!”

Everyone wanted to see. The students crowded around Abby and the cage, elbowing each other to get closer.

“Mrs. Nibbles had her puppies in my exercise ball,” Rachel said proudly. She flashed Abby a thumbs-up sign.

“I had no idea he was a she,” murmured Mrs. Hernandez.

Abby had done some research. She cleared her throat importantly. “Teddy bear hamsters have a gestation period of sixteen days. That means it’s sixteen days before the babies are ready to be born. So Mrs. Nibbles was already pregnant when she came to live in our classroom.”

Abby looked around to see if everyone was listening. “There were lots of clues that she was pregnant,” she continued. “For one thing, she was really chubby.” Abby thought of Tess.

"Someone told me she was fat, but I didn't listen. Another clue was her appetite. She ate and ate and ate. The fatter she got, the hungrier she seemed. The last clue was her personality. When she came to stay at my house, all of a sudden she didn't like me. She wouldn't let me touch her. She acted like an entirely different hamster."

Abby paused for breath and beamed at the class. "So now we have a whole bunch of class pets."

Some of the kids clapped and cheered. Mrs. Hernandez shook her head in amazement. "Well, I have to say, this is a real turn of events. I'm certainly glad our class pet was in such good hands over spring break. I don't know how we can properly thank you."

Abby grinned. She had been hoping Mrs. Hernandez would say that. She leaned forward and whispered something in her teacher's ear. After a moment, Mrs. Hernandez nodded in agreement.

Abby kept her secret all day. When the

last bell rang she stuffed her homework into her backpack and went to meet her sister outside. Tess stood near the flagpole, wearing the same hangdog expression she'd had on that morning.

Abby smiled at her. "Hi Tess, how was your day?"

Tess shrugged. "Okay, I guess. Did they like our hamsters?"

"Yup," Abby replied. "Nobody could believe their eyes when I took the towel off. It was awesome."

"Great," said Tess listlessly.

They started walking home. "It's too bad Mr. Brewster had to come back," Abby said innocently. "Desmond probably would've let us keep one of the puppies."

Tess looked even sadder. "Yeah."

Abby shrugged. "Oh well, having a class pet is the next best thing. Don't you think?"

Tess nodded, but didn't speak.

Abby could barely contain herself. "So which one do you think you'll pick?"

Tess stopped walking and stared at Abby. "Huh?"

Abby stopped too, pretending not to notice Tess's confusion. "Which one do you think you'll pick?" she repeated. "I bet you'll take the dark brown one. He's going to be the furriest, I think. But maybe you'd rather have that cream-colored one with the white feet. Anyway, it's up to you."

"What are you talking about?" demanded Tess. She stared at her sister as though she'd suddenly lost her mind.

Abby laughed out loud. "I knew how much you were going to miss having those hamsters on our dresser, so I talked to Mrs. Hernandez. She thinks it's a great idea for your class to have a class pet too. And since you did most of the pet-sitting, I thought you should be the one to choose it. You get to name it too."

"Wow," whispered Tess. Abby's words were beginning to sink in. "Really?"

"Sure. Except the puppies can't leave their mother just yet. They won't be old enough for another two weeks. But that'll give your class time to raise money for a cage and food and stuff."

Tess let out a joyful yelp and threw herself at Abby. Laughing, Abby tried to dodge her wet doggy kisses. Finally she gave Tess a quick hug, glancing around the playground to make sure no one was watching.

They started walking again, only this time there was a bounce in Tess's step. She barked happily at every person they passed. They were almost at the steps of their apartment building when Tess stopped dead in her tracks.

"I still have a problem," she giggled.

"What?" asked Abby, puzzled. Everything had worked out perfectly.

Tess cocked her head to one side and stared at her sister. "I won't know whether to name it Henry or Henrietta!"